BEYOND REFRACTED LIGHT

Lopez

First Edition MMXXV

Printed in the United States of America

ISBN: 979-8-9937359-2-4

Cover design by: Author

Interior design by: Author

Published by Veiled Truths Press

www.thelopezbooks.com

For you.

Who made something unreal—feel real.

Static

The rain had been falling for three days straight. Not a storm. Not a downpour. Just a steady, colorless curtain that blurred the edges of the city into something tired and unfinished.

Evan Reyes sat on his cracked leather couch in a room that smelled faintly of damp paper and rust. The television murmured without conviction. Cold coffee rested in his grip, forgotten. The mug had a chip in the handle—he rubbed it with his thumb like a worry stone.

The news anchor's voice carried the weight of routine tragedy.

"...taken off life support after six months in a coma. Doctors citing irreversible brain damage. Jobes Family gathered to say their final goodbyes…"

Evan clicked the TV off. The room fell into a deeper silence, thickened by the tick of the kitchen clock and the quiet hum of a dying refrigerator.

He watched his reflection on the dark screen: hunched, unshaven, and older than he remembered. His fingers drifted to the thin gold chain at his neck—the one his abuelita had pressed into his palm just before her last breath. He still wore it. Always had.

The call pulsed once on the wall display. Evan didn't move.

It rang again.

And again.

On the fourth pulse, the system answered for him.

"You've reached Evan. If it matters, you know what to do."

A soft tone followed.

"Evan… hermanito, it's your big sis. I'm worried about you. I know abuelita's passing was tough. I'm here, okay? Please… just call me back. I mean it."

The silence settled like dust.

He stood.

The apartment shifted around him—floorboards creaking, walls exhaling, a place built more on memory than maintenance. He pulled his jacket from the hook. It smelled of old smoke and older rain.

On the counter, beside his wallet, lay the Echo Room access pass. Faded plastic. Corners curled. He picked it up and turned it over in his fingers.

Tomorrow, he had told himself.

But tomorrow was just another way to say never.

He pocketed the pass, opened the door, and stepped into the gray.

The rain greeted him like it always did—patient, unfeeling.

He walked.

Not toward hope. Not toward purpose. Just forward.

Toward the only place where colors still remembered how to dream.

Beneath a Colorless Sky

The rain was less a storm now and more a habit—drizzling from a sky too tired to choose.

Evan moved down Soto Street with his hood drawn low, hands in his pockets, head down. The city didn't speak anymore. It sighed.

Men slumped at bus stops that hadn't worked in years. Women hauled bags through puddles the color of engine oil. Kids sat with their backs to crumbling walls, faces bathed in blue light, fingers swiping at nothing.

No one looked at him. No one looked at anyone. It wasn't that they didn't see. It was that they had stopped expecting to be seen.

A preacher barked half-verses from a milk crate. Something about fire and judgment. His voice disappeared into the wet hush of tires and failing engines.

Evan passed beneath a tired neon sign that buzzed above the sidewalk like a dying insect.

HONOR & HOPE, it once said.

Now the HO in HONOR was dead. The R flickered once, like it remembered its name, and went dark. The ampersand blinked like a slow pulse, then nothing.

NO HOPE.

It hung there, humming in the drizzle. Reflected in the puddles. Burned into concrete like prophecy.

Evan looked up, not surprised. Not sad. Just... aligned. The sign wasn't wrong.

He moved on.

At the corner of Soto and Olympic, the old Sears building rose like a stone ghost. Cracked facade. Windows like hollow eyes. What used to be department stores and catalog counters now held only echoes.

And one door still lit.

The Echo Room pulsed faintly behind fractured glass. The only color left in the world that wasn't rust or neon or memory.

Evan approached the door.

And behind him, the city kept pretending it was alive.

Entry

The doors creaked open on hydraulic hinges, spilling Evan into a gutted lobby soaked in cold fluorescent light.

The rain clung to his jacket, dripping onto cracked tile floors where faded outlines of old Sears logos still ghosted beneath layers of grime.

The place should have been silent.

Forgotten.

But it wasn't.

A holographic attendant flickered into existence just beyond the threshold—a woman, polished to the point of parody, with too-white teeth and eyes that never quite blinked.

"Welcome to the Echo Room!"

"A NuroTech experience"

"We're thrilled to guide you toward your perfect day!"

Her voice was a sugary weapon.

High, lilting, almost musical — the kind of corporate enthusiasm designed to erase sadness through repetition.

Evan didn't answer.

He kept walking, boots tapping hollow echoes through the dead lobby.

"Please proceed to your personal chamber at your earliest convenience!"

"Thank you for choosing the Echo Room! Your dreams are waiting!"

"My pleasure to assist you, Mr. Reyes!"

The last line followed him like static.

He moved past faded wayfinding signs until he reached the access hallway — lined with glass booths like vertical coffins.

Each booth pulsed faintly with dormant light, waiting for someone foolish enough to climb inside.

He picked an empty chamber at random.

No lines. There were never lines anymore.

Stepping inside, he turned and pulled the door closed behind him.

It sealed with a pneumatic sigh, cutting off the noise of the lobby like a blade slicing through fabric.

Silence.

Perfect, suffocating silence.

For a long moment, Evan simply stood there.

The chamber was small enough that he could touch both walls if he stretched his arms out —

bare concrete floor, frosted panels.

Nothing human left in it.

Then, from the center of the booth, a thin shimmer bloomed outward.

A floating holographic panel stitched itself together midair, lines of soft blue static weaving a fragile screen.

"Voice command recognized."

"Please state destination archive."

The voice was different now.

Colder.

Neutral.

All customer service smiles were left in the lobby.

Evan cleared his throat —

a rasp like broken paper.

"Load file," he said.

"East L.A. Archive zero zero two."

A faint chime.

Confirmation.

The floor beneath him trembled softly, the panels bleeding away into light.

Colors, muted at first, trickled into the corners of his vision—like a long-forgotten watercolor reawakening.

The ceiling peeled away to reveal a soft, endless blue sky.

The walls blurred into streets lined with palm trees, taco stands, old lowriders gleaming under a resurrected sun.

Buildings wore fresh paint; murals danced on brickwork like the city was alive again.

He took a step forward.

The rain was gone.

The grey was gone.

The hollow ache in his ribs softened — not gone, never gone, but smothered under layers of color and light.

He let himself breathe.

Somewhere nearby, in the bright resurrection of a Boyle Heights that never truly existed,

a voice brushed past his ear.

Soft.

Familiar.

Almost... real.

He turned toward the sound —

but there was nothing.

Only sunlight dripping through imagined trees.

Only a memory that hadn't been his in years.

Evan Reyes adjusted his jacket, stepped onto the conjured street,

and disappeared into the dream.

Rosa

Evan walked deeper into the simulation. The city responded to him, not like a mirror, but like a memory given rhythm and light. The murals bloomed brighter when he passed. The smell of grilled meat sharpened. Every alley felt like home, repainted.

A bolero drifted from an open window, wrapping around him like something forgotten but cherished. The taco stand on Fickett was still there. Fresh paint, full menu. A boy wiped the counter. A dog waited beside a crate of Jarritos.

And then—her.

Sitting on a bench just past the bakery, beneath the branches of a jacaranda tree. The petals scattered around her like someone had arranged them by hand.

Her smile was the first thing he noticed. Easy. Warm. Not performed.

Then her eyes—dark, curious, steady. They held his gaze without challenge.

A breeze stirred and she lifted a hand to tuck a strand of hair behind her ear. It was a delicate motion, and for a moment, Evan forgot to breathe.

Her skin caught the filtered sunlight with a warm, toasted glow. At her neck, a thin gold necklace rested in the hollow above her collarbone. She wore a sundress, light and simple, shaped to her petite silhouette like it had been made for this day.

Her fingers, as she closed the book in her lap, were graceful. A French manicure—subtle but elegant.

And then she laughed.

Soft. Effortless. The kind of sound that makes flowers grow.

Evan stood there, stunned. Not enchanted. Not bewitched.

Drawn.

Like a moth recognizing the flame as home.

She looked up at him as if she'd known him forever.

"Nice day, huh?"

Evan found his voice. "Yeah… it is."

She studied him for a second longer than most people would. Not uncomfortable. Just… curious.

"People forget how to look up," she said. "Even when it's right there."

Evan glanced at the sky, then back at her. "Guess I'm one of the few, then."

A faint smile touched her lips. "Maybe."

She patted the bench beside her. "Sit for a minute. I was just about to walk, but I like the company."

He hesitated—just long enough to notice it.

Then nodded, heart climbing into his throat, and sat.

She didn't introduce herself immediately. There was no need.

Instead, she looked out at the street like she was listening to something deeper than the noise.

Eventually, she said, "I'm Rosa."

"Evan."

She nodded, like she was placing the name somewhere.

"I like that name."

He let out a quiet breath. "Yeah?"

"It sounds like someone who notices things."

Evan almost laughed. "You don't even know me."

Rosa tilted her head slightly.

"I think I do."

They sat in silence for a beat.

And then she stood, offered her hand.

"Come walk with me."

And he did.

Patterns

Evan didn't bother with coffee the next morning. He didn't shave. Didn't check the time. The day moved around him like scenery behind glass.

He left the apartment in silence, card in his pocket, rain on his hood. The city said nothing. He didn't answer.

The bus ride blurred.

Faces came and went. Stops were announced. Doors hissed open and shut.

Evan watched the window more than anything else.

Rain smeared the world into streaks of gray and light.

For a moment, the glass caught something warmer—

gold, almost—

then it slipped away with the motion of the street.

By the time he stepped off, he couldn't remember the ride.

`<DIR>...`

The warehouse hummed with fluorescent fatigue.

Evan stacked boxes without really seeing them. His hands moved on memory. His mind didn't.

"Yo."

He didn't respond.

"Yo—Evan."

A hand tapped the side of a pallet. He blinked, like surfacing.

Marcus stood there, one eyebrow raised.

"You good, bro?"

Evan nodded too quickly. "Yeah. Yeah, I'm good."

Marcus didn't move. Just watched him for a second.

"You been saying that a lot lately."

Evan shrugged, already reaching for another box. "Work, man."

Marcus leaned against the forklift, not convinced.

"Yeah… work."

A beat.

Then he clapped Evan lightly on the shoulder.

"Aight. Just don't get lost in that head of yours, yeah?"

Evan gave a half-smile. "I'll try."

Marcus held his gaze a second longer—like he almost had something else to say.

Then thought better of it.

"Break in ten," he said, hopping back onto the forklift.

The machine whined to life and rolled away.

Evan stood there for a moment.

Then picked up the next box.

<DIR>...

In the breakroom, the coffee machine hissed like it was tired of trying.

Evan stood by the window, paper cup in hand.

Rain streaked the glass in uneven lines.

For a second—

the reflection shifted.

Light broke across it. Warm. Golden.

Like sunlight.

He blinked.

It was gone.

Just gray.

Just rain.

He didn't finish the coffee.

He stood there a moment longer, watching the glass like it might do it again.

It didn't.

Just gray. Just rain.

His thumb brushed the card in his pocket.

Warm.

He didn't think about it.

He went.

Inside the Echo Room, the light welcomed him like a memory waiting to be touched again. His booth opened with a soft chime. Familiar.

When the simulation loaded, she was there.

Rosa.

Same bench, different dress. Pale yellow. It suited her.

She smiled when she saw him—

"You took a little longer today."

Not like a program greeting a user, but like someone glad to see a friend again. Or something more.

They walked. She asked him questions. Told him stories that didn't seem prewritten.

"Tell me about your abuelita," she said once.

He did. About the mercado. The songs she hummed when she cleaned. The red thread she tied around his wrist as a kid.

As he spoke, the world listened.

Rosa watched him for a moment, quieter now.

"You were thinking about her earlier," she said. "On the bus."

Evan frowned slightly. "Yeah… I guess."

The simulation shimmered—not glitched, but adapted. A vendor two blocks down began humming that same tune. The color of the house across the street shifted to match his grandmother's faded green.

He didn't say anything.

But he noticed.

And the next day, it happened again.

He came back. Again.

Again.

Again.

Each time, Rosa was there. A different dress. A new story. She remembered things he'd told her once, even things he'd forgotten.

"I like that you always notice the sky," she said.

He didn't remember telling her that.

He stopped eating. Started forgetting to turn off lights. Spoke to no one. There was no reason to.

In the Echo Room, Rosa laughed. She held his hand once. Not out of romance—but because it felt right.

Her fingers were warm. Or they felt warm. He didn't care which it was.

When he left that day, the sky outside was a slab of wet steel. His apartment was smaller than he remembered. Darker.

The smell of damp carpet hit him harder than it should have.

He stood in the kitchen for a while, unsure why he'd come back at all.

That night, he lay on his mattress, staring at the ceiling fan that no longer spun.

Her smile. The light in her eyes. The sound of her laugh.

The shape of her breasts.

Every part of her etched into him like a song he couldn't stop humming.

He whispered her name like a secret.

"Rosa."

Cracks in the World

Evan woke to gray light spilling through his curtains, filtered through rain-spattered glass. The kind of light that made everything look older. Dustier.

He sat up slowly. His head felt thick. He looked around the apartment—cluttered table, overflowing trash bin, coffee mugs stained to the rim. On the floor near the door: a folded slip of paper. A shutoff notice. Electric or water. He didn't check which.

The fridge buzzed louder than usual. Or maybe it always had. Maybe he was just hearing things now. Really hearing them.

He walked into the bathroom and stared into the mirror. His face was softer somehow. Paler. As if it had forgotten the sun.

"You look like someone waiting to disappear," he muttered.

The handset on the counter pulsed once.

His sister again.

He didn't answer. Let it go to voicemail.

He didn't listen right away. Just stared at the blinking light.

Eventually, curiosity won.

He let it play.

"Evan? It's me. I don't know if you even check this anymore. You've been… off the radar. People are worried. I'm worried. Whatever's going on… don't let it swallow you. Okay? I know you're in there. Wherever 'there' is."

He deleted it before the voice could say goodbye.

He put on the same jacket. Same boots. Walked the same cracked sidewalk to the corner store.

Inside, the fluorescent lights stung his eyes. The cashier looked half-asleep. Evan grabbed a bottle of water, a pack of instant noodles.

His card declined.

He tried again. Same result. The cashier didn't say anything. Just waited.

Evan put the items back and left.

Outside, a man screamed at pigeons. A little girl screamed at her mother. No one seemed to hear either of them. The rain returned—more of a mist than a storm, but it settled on his skin like judgment.

He didn't go home.

He went where it felt safe.

The Echo Room greeted him with soft light. No questions.

Inside the chamber, he didn't even have to speak anymore. It remembered.

East L.A. Archive 002.

The dream spun back into place.

Rosa was waiting. On a different bench this time. Pale yellow dress. Bare feet.

Her smile made something inside him unclench.

"You're late," she teased.

"I didn't know I was supposed to be on time."

"You're not. I just missed you."

They walked without destination, weaving through a sun-drenched street that didn't exist. Murals blinked alive as they passed. Music drifted from balconies. Wind stirred her dress just enough to catch the gold chain at her neck.

"I used to climb onto the roof to watch the sky turn gold," Rosa said.

Evan looked at her. "When?"

"Before."

"Before what?"

She tilted her head. "Maybe before I knew what I was."

"Do you know now?"

"Sometimes."

Evan held her gaze a second longer than he meant to

They didn't speak after that. Not because there was nothing to say—but because silence felt realer than words.

When the session ended, Evan stood in the booth longer than he meant to. Rosa's voice lingered as the simulation dimmed.

"Will you come back tomorrow?"

He didn't answer. Just nodded. Once.

Outside, the city hadn't changed. The smell of wet concrete. The hiss of tires. Someone yelling far away.

Evan didn't know what day it was anymore.

Didn't care.

He walked home, left the lights off, didn't lock the door behind him.

What was the point?

Expiration Date

It was the most beautiful day yet.

The simulated sun spilled honey across the rooftops. The air felt cool but sweet, touched with the smell of gardenias and grilled corn. Somewhere nearby, a record played an old love song in Spanish—one Evan couldn't name but felt like he'd danced to in another life.

Rosa greeted him on the steps of a mural-covered courtyard he didn't remember selecting. Her dress was the color of apricots. She held two paletas in her hands, one already melting.

"For you," she said.

He laughed and took it.

"You planned this?"

"I dreamed it."

They walked through streets more alive than they'd ever been. Children played in the spray of a busted hydrant. A mural blinked and changed shape when Rosa looked at it. A dog barked in rhythm with the music.

The sky melted into the horizon like stained glass.

But then—

A bird paused mid-flight, hanging there, wings outstretched.

A flower near the bakery bloomed, closed—then bloomed again.

And Rosa—just for a second—winced. Like something was pushing too hard against her.

Evan said nothing. The moment passed. The bird resumed its flight. The flower wilted into stillness.

"Are you okay?" he asked.

She looked confused. "Of course.

Why wouldn't I be?"

He smiled. Too quickly. "Just making sure."

They walked until the sun dipped low, casting the city in cinematic light.

At the exit gate, she touched his wrist.

"Don't stay away too long."

"I won't."

But just as the booth began its logout sequence, the holographic attendant appeared—superimposed over Rosa's fading form.

NOTICE: ECHO ROOM ARCHIVE 002
SCHEDULED FOR SUNSET DECOMMISSION.
THIS SIMULATION WILL BE PERMANENTLY
RETIRED.

The voice was flat. Cold.

The message looped twice, then vanished.

Rosa was gone.

Evan stood alone in the booth, staring into a light that no longer felt warm.

At home, he didn't turn on the lights.

He opened his laptop. The Echo Room portal rejected his login.

He tried a backdoor—an old employee portal someone once showed him.

Access denied.

He called customer service. Got a looped message: "Your experience matters to us. Please stay on the line."

He stayed on the line for twenty-three minutes.

Then hung up.

The next day, Rosa met him at the fountain downtown. Simulated, of course. She was barefoot again.

"You seem off," she said.

"I didn't sleep."

"Why not?"

He paused.

"Because I don't know what's real anymore."

She looked at him. Not confused. Just quiet.

"Do you think I'm real?" she asked.

He didn't answer. Not with words.

Instead he said, "What do you dream about?"

She smiled.

"Color. Music. People I don't know but feel familiar. Sometimes I dream you're watching me…

but I'm not here. And I miss you."

He wanted to cry. But he didn't.

She took his hand.

"Will you be here tomorrow?"

"Of course," he said.

When he returned to the booth the next day, a red icon blinked in the corner of the screen.

ARCHIVE CLOSURE: 6 DAYS REMAINING

Rosa waved to him across a street filled with light.

She didn't seem to notice the countdown.

But Evan did.

And for the first time, it felt like the world could end without him.

The Back Door

The forums were dead.

Buried under layers of ghost code, obsolete threads, and user handles long abandoned. Evan dug through them anyway—hour after hour, night bleeding into day, room lit only by the screen's electric hum.

He searched for anything: legacy access, neural mapping, quantum mirroring, black site simulation nodes. Keywords whispered across broken threads.

Most were junk. Conspiracy garbage. Schizophrenic manifesto-level nonsense.

But not all.

Three separate users mentioned the same name in different years, different contexts.

IrisBurn.

No name. No location. Just fragments:

"ran backend on the Echo Room before the lockout"

"walked out with a dev build that could kill you if you blinked wrong"

"they say he mapped himself once… and didn't come back whole"

Evan copied what he could. Thread IDs. Access logs. A burner contact string that hadn't been pinged in over a year.

He sent a message anyway.

The reply came two hours later.

A single line: Bring something real.

The warehouse was at the city's edge, where the infrastructure forgot to keep breathing. Broken windows. Graffiti curling like vines. Metal doors scarred with old fire.

Evan stood outside for a full minute before pressing the buzzer.

A camera above the door twitched, adjusting. Focusing.

A voice crackled through a speaker.

"Who is it?"

It sounded like he was eating.

"Evan."

A long pause.

Then—

BUZZ.

The steel door unlocked with a mechanical hiss.

Inside, it was a graveyard of machines—CRT monitors, servers blinking like dying hearts, wires looping like veins from wall to wall. The smell was copper and ozone.

IrisBurn sat behind a desk that looked welded from scrap. Pale, unshaven, and lit by a flickering screen. His left eye was artificial—old tech, a flickering green iris that twitched when he blinked.

"You're Evan." He chewed from a crinkled bag of Turtle chips.

"Yeah."

"You want out."

Evan hesitated.

"I want in."

IrisBurn grinned, all teeth and ruin. "Same thing."

He stood and moved toward a terminal. Dragged a portable rig the size of a briefcase out from under the table.

"This is a mirror node. It hijacks Echo Room architecture and reroutes the transfer through your frontal cortex. No corporate interface. No regulatory caps. Just you, the quantum mesh, and whatever version of you gets digitized."

Evan stared at the machine. It looked like it had been built in a basement by someone on the run. Probably had.

"What happens to my body?"

"It dies," IrisBurn said flatly.

"Eventually. Maybe immediately."

He shrugged.

"Depends on how much of you it decides to keep."

Evan didn't flinch.

IrisBurn watched him.

"I've had five ask me for this in the last three years. One changed his mind. Three are buried. One's still in there, far as I know. Keeps trying to convince himself he's happy."

Evan asked, "What does it cost?"

IrisBurn reached under the table and pulled out an old photo scanner.

"Memory. One you've never told anyone. Something too real for the machine to fake. You give that up, the system gives you a space to hold onto."

Evan swallowed.

He reached into his wallet. Pulled out a folded photo—his abuelita. Holding him as a boy, wearing the red thread bracelet, sunlight caught in her hair.

IrisBurn didn't take it. Just nodded.

"When do we start?"

"When you stop being afraid to die."

He turned away. The screen behind him came alive, scrolling code like it had been waiting.

Evan sat down in the chair across from it.

And for the first time since he met Rosa—he didn't feel warm.

He felt cold.

Like something in him had already begun to leave.

The Plea

Rosa wasn't at the fountain. Not at the taco stand. Not on the bench beneath the jacaranda tree.

Evan wandered deeper into the archive. The sky stayed the same—perfectly blue, perfectly still—but the quiet felt different. Like something was holding its breath.

He found her sitting alone at the edge of a simulated bluff, just beyond the mural garden. Her feet dangled over a steep drop that faded into soft mist. She didn't turn when he approached.

"It feels thinner today," she said.

He sat beside her. "The sky?"

She nodded. "Like something's pressing down on it. Like it's trying to hold back a storm that already passed."

They sat in silence. The wind moved through her hair like it remembered how. Her dress rippled across her knees.

"I thought I lost you," he said.

"You don't lose things that don't belong to you."

He looked at her. "Is that what you are?"

She shrugged. "I don't know what I am."

He reached out, took her hand. Her fingers curled around his like they had weight. Warmth. Memory.

"I've been thinking," he said.

"You've been deciding."

He froze. She turned to him.

"What did you do?"

"Nothing," he lied.

Rosa pulled her hand back.

"Evan."

He looked away.

"I just—" he started. "I don't want to lose this. You. Any of it. Out there, I wake up and everything feels like static. Here, it's like… color. Like breath."

She said nothing.

"So I found a way," he whispered. "A way to stay."

The silence that followed wasn't artificial. It was the kind that fills a cathedral when the last candle dies.

"You'd die… for me?"

He didn't answer.

She turned her face toward the sun. It made the gold chain at her neck catch fire.

"I don't know how I got here," she said. "Sometimes I remember things—places I've never seen, people I've never met. I think maybe I was made from someone else's grief.

Maybe from yours."

Her voice cracked—not glitched, not coded. Just soft.

"I don't dream like you do. I only have pieces. But you… if you cross over, you won't be you. You'll be… something else. And I don't know if I'll recognize you anymore."

56

She wiped her cheek.

Nothing was there.

Evan reached for her but stopped. His hand hovered above her shoulder.

"I can't lose you," he said.

"You can't keep losing yourself to find me," she said back.

They sat like that until the sun began to set in soft, looping colors.

A mural across the street blinked, froze for half a second, then resumed its motion.

Rosa leaned into him.

"I don't want to lose you."

"I think I already have," he whispered.

And neither of them spoke again.

The world held.

Descent

The apartment was silent when Evan woke. No hum of the fridge. No flicker from the thermostat.

The power was out. The world had followed through on its final threat.

He didn't check the handset. The blinking light meant someone still cared. But it didn't matter now.

He walked to the drawer near the kitchen sink. Inside, like relics waiting for their ritual, were the Echo Room access card, IrisBurn's portable node, and a folded photo of his abuelita.

He held the photo a long time. His thumb traced her face. The smile. The sunlight caught in her hair. Then, slowly, he flipped it over and set it face-down.

It was time.

<DIR>...

IrisBurn didn't say much when Evan arrived.

The warehouse looked different in daylight. Less like a lair. More like a mausoleum. Dust floated in shafts of light. The cables across the floor seemed to twitch like nerves.

The rig was already active. The mirror node buzzed like a swarm.

"You sure?" IrisBurn asked, though his hands were already moving.

"I left a while ago," Evan said.

IrisBurn nodded. "You'll go under fast. You'll feel cold. Like dying, but backward. Focus on where you want to wake up. That becomes your anchor."

He strapped the leads to Evan's temples. The chair reclined. The lights dimmed.

"When you cross," IrisBurn said, "you can't drag anything with you. No past. No skin. Just pattern."

"I'm ready."

The machine hissed to life. Code crawled across the monitor like vines on a headstone.

Evan felt it immediately—the tug. Like something beneath his ribs was being pulled into a smaller, brighter space.

His breath grew shallow. The walls blurred. He couldn't feel his hands.

Then, Rosa's voice.

Not from the room. From inside.

"You said you wouldn't leave."

"I'm not," he whispered.

The light above him flickered. His heartbeat slowed.

He closed his eyes and pictured her. The smile. The warmth. The gold chain around her neck catching the light.

IrisBurn's voice, distant now:

"Focus."

And then—nothing.

No breath. No body.

A breeze.

Sunlight.

The smell of jacaranda blossoms.

Evan opened his eyes beneath a purple-leafed tree. The world shimmered softly around him. Gentle. Diffuse.

Rosa was sitting nearby, exactly where she always had been. Or almost.

"You're late," she said, smiling.

He exhaled. Smiled back.

"I'm here."

She stood, took his hand.

The city pulsed with light around them. Slower now. Like a memory replaying just under speed.

A mural flickered, briefly.

Behind Rosa's eyes—just for a second—a glint of red. Like a warning.

Gone as quickly as it came.

She squeezed his hand. "Come on. Let's walk."

And Evan followed her into the dream.

Never noticing the red icon in the sky.

Blinking.

ARCHIVE LOCKDOWN INITIATED

Ghostlight

The world was quiet now.

Not dead. Not broken. Just... slowing.

Evan walked beside Rosa through the soft dusk of the archive. The sun no longer rose or fell—it just hung there, like a lantern left on for someone who might return.

They moved through streets overtaken by jacaranda blossoms and silence. Murals faded at the edges, like watercolors left in the rain. Music still played from somewhere, but it was distant. Hollow. A melody remembered more than performed.

Rosa hummed along without knowing the words.

"Does it feel different?" Evan asked.

She nodded. "Everything moves like it's remembering how. Like it's trying to keep up with us."

They passed the fountain, now dry. The corner stand no longer served paletas. The color was still there—but subdued. Faded like dreams after waking.

"This place is winding down," Rosa said.

"I know."

They didn't mourn it. They kept walking.

Later, beneath the gold-drenched sky, they sat on a rooftop overlooking the mural district. Rosa leaned against Evan's shoulder.

"I used to think I was just a reflection," she said. "A collection of everything you wanted. But now... I don't think I'm yours anymore."

He looked at her.

She smiled.

"I think I'm mine."

He reached for her hand. "Even if that's true... you're still what I choose."

She closed her eyes.

"I remember the moment you looked at me like I mattered. I think that's when I began."

A distant vibration trembled beneath them. The skyline flickered—not violently, just a soft warning.

Above the rooftops, a shifting aurora spread like fractured glass, red and violet woven into the clouds.

Neither of them looked at it for long.

"Do you think we'll know when it ends?" Evan asked.

Rosa shook her head. "Not if we keep moving."

They walked to a hill that hadn't been there before. The city behind them melted into soft gradients. Trees leaned toward the light. The wind carried nothing but warmth.

In the grass, Rosa slipped the chain from her neck. The gold shimmered faintly in the open air.

She placed it in Evan's palm.

"If we forget," she said, "maybe this will remember."

He closed his hand around it.

Together, they stepped forward.

The light ahead wasn't bright.

Not at first.

It flickered—subtle, like something trying to stabilize.

Rosa's hand tightened in his. Just a little too much.

Evan didn't react.

They kept walking.

The world softened around them. Edges dissolving. Color bleeding into white.

Not as code. Not as ghosts.

Just… them.

The light swallowed everything.

Then, in the upper corner—barely there—

a red icon blinked.

Once.

And again.

[ARCHIVE STABILITY: UNDEFINED]

█

Epilogue

[LOG ENTRY - CORRUPTED]

...

...signal detected...

...pattern incomplete...

...attempting reconstruction...

...█

About the Author

Lopez is a multidisciplinary creator whose work blends with gritty realism, philosophical undertones, and raw emotion. Being an entrepreneur, gunsmith, leather craftsman and writer, his storytelling spans fiction, design, and social commentary.

He is the founder of Veiled Truths Press and when not writing, you can find him customizing firearms, making leather goods, or working in his Southern California workshop.

Connect with him:

www.thelopezbooks.com

@kingdom05

Kingmsgot.substack.com

Also by Lopez

Veiled Truths: The Lucian Graves Mysteries Vol's 1-3

A trilogy exploring secrets, survival, and the cost of clarity.

Interim

A haunting blend of noir and psychological suspense.

The Witnesses: The Fall of Eden

A cosmic reckoning that challenges the fate of humanity.

The Blood of the Son: A cartel family saga

A story of the consequences of a sons decisions for the love of his father.